# How I Became a Pirate

# How I Became a Pirate

WRITTEN BY
## Melinda Long

ILLUSTRATED BY
## David Shannon

## Harcourt, Inc.

Orlando  Austin  New York  San Diego  Toronto  London

Printed in Singapore

Pirates have green teeth—when they have any teeth at all. I know about pirates, because one day, when I was at the beach building a sand castle and minding my own business, a pirate ship sailed into view. I knew what it was, because its flag had a skull and crossbones on it and because I could hear the pirates singing, "Hey, ho, blow the man down." They were a little off-key.

I tried to tell Dad, but he was busy setting up the beach umbrella. I tried to tell Mom, but she was busy slathering my baby sister with sunblock.

So I went back to my sand castle, but I kept an eye on the pirates. By then they were rowing to shore.

When they landed, the head pirate climbed out of the boat
and yelled, "Ahoy thar, matey! Be this the Spanish Main?"
"No," I said, "this is North Beach."
"Shiver me timbers!" the pirate said. "We must have taken
a wrong turn at Bora Bora."

He walked around my sand castle. He looked at the moat, then yelled back to his crew. "He's a digger, he is, and a good one to boot!"

"A good one to boot!"

the others agreed.

"What be your name, matey?" the head pirate asked.

"Jeremy Jacob, sir," I told him.

"Well, Jeremy Jacob," he said, "you're lookin' at Braid Beard and his crew. We've been needin' a digger like yourself. We've a chest of treasure to bury."

# "Aye! Treasure!"

the others shouted.

"You're comin' with us!" Braid Beard told me.

I didn't think Mom and Dad would mind, as long as I got back in time for soccer practice the next day.

That's how I became a pirate.

As soon as we were on board, Braid Beard showed me
the chest of gold and jewels. "Got to find a safe place for this
here treasure. It's high time we were off!" he announced.

"We're off!" we all shouted.

And then we set sail.

There was plenty to do on board. The pirates taught me to sing sea chanteys—the louder, the better. And to say real pirate stuff like "landlubber" and "scurvy dog." By dinnertime, I could speak pirate perfectly.

I also learned pirate manners. Braid Beard pounded his fist on the table and yelled, "Down the hatch, me laddies!"

"Down the hatch!"

we all shouted.

Braid Beard gulped his food and said, "Hand over the meat!"

"The meat!" we all roared.

Nobody told us to finish our spinach (there wasn't any) or to chew up our carrots (they weren't allowed on board). We talked with our mouths full. And *nobody* said "please" or "thank you."

After dinner I tried to teach the pirates to play soccer. Braid Beard kicked the ball and yelled, "Aargh! Soccer!"

"Aargh! Soccer!"

the crew yelled.

Then everybody dove for the ball at once, and it rolled right off the deck.

"After it, me hearties!" Braid Beard commanded.

"After it?" we all whispered.

We fought over who would go get the ball. But it didn't matter anyway, because a shark came along and swallowed it in one gulp. So much for soccer.

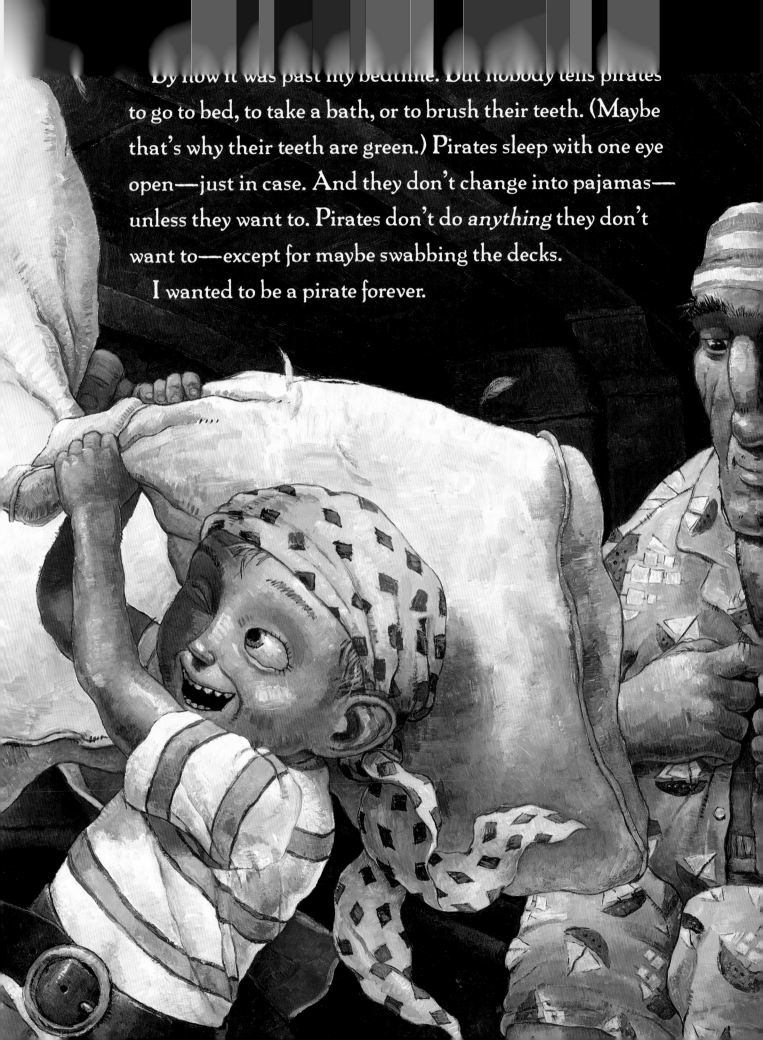

By now it was past my bedtime. But nobody tells pirates to go to bed, to take a bath, or to brush their teeth. (Maybe that's why their teeth are green.) Pirates sleep with one eye open—just in case. And they don't change into pajamas—unless they want to. Pirates don't do *anything* they don't want to—except for maybe swabbing the decks.

I wanted to be a pirate forever.

But then I found out what else they don't do.

When I couldn't stay awake any longer, I asked

Braid Beard to tuck me in and read me a story.

"Tuck you in?" he bellowed. "Pirates don't tuck."

# "No tucking!"

the crew cried.

And the only thing they had to read was a map.

"Don't you have any books?" I asked.

Braid Beard looked confused. "Books?"

I didn't even bother to ask about a good-night kiss.

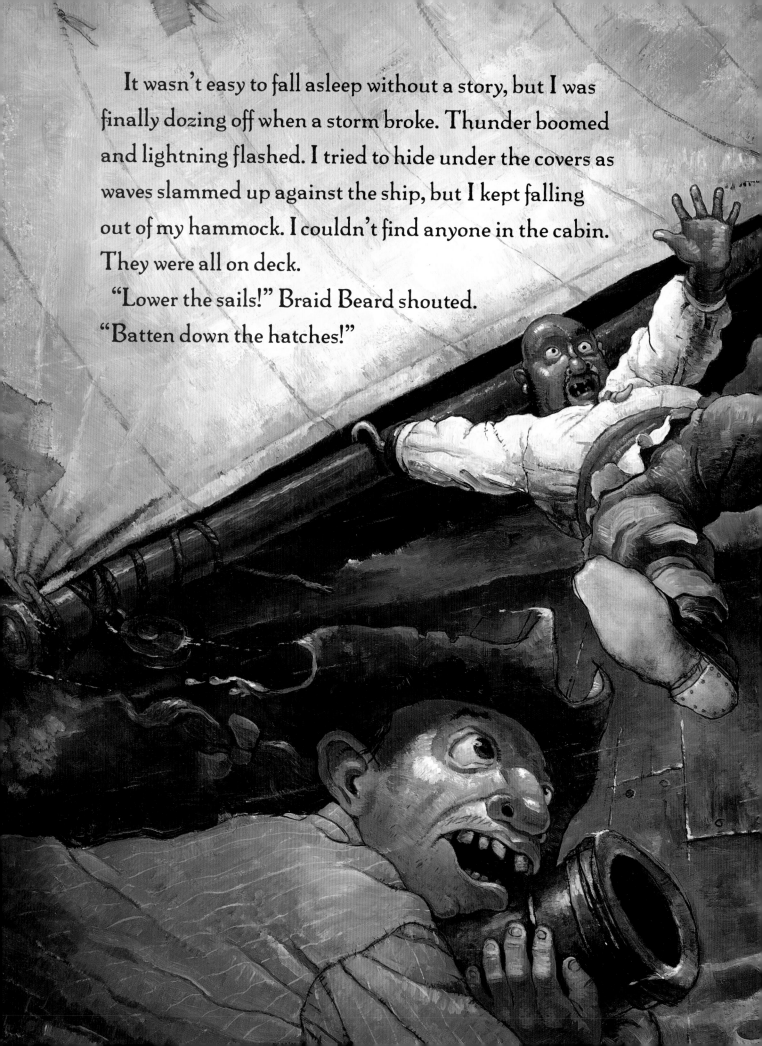

It wasn't easy to fall asleep without a story, but I was finally dozing off when a storm broke. Thunder boomed and lightning flashed. I tried to hide under the covers as waves slammed up against the ship, but I kept falling out of my hammock. I couldn't find anyone in the cabin. They were all on deck.

"Lower the sails!" Braid Beard shouted. "Batten down the hatches!"

Everybody ran around yelling and lowering and battening.
Nobody had time to sit close and tell me it would be over soon.
Nobody even noticed me.
I decided that I didn't want to be a pirate after all.

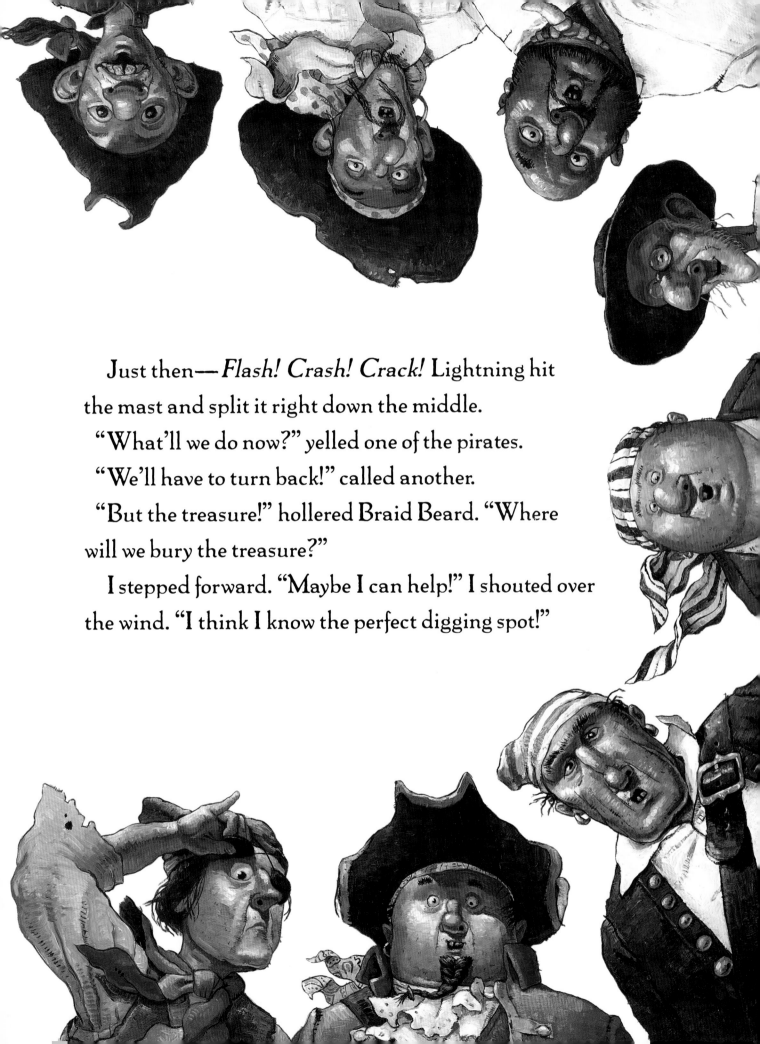

Just then—*Flash! Crash! Crack!* Lightning hit
the mast and split it right down the middle.

"What'll we do now?" yelled one of the pirates.

"We'll have to turn back!" called another.

"But the treasure!" hollered Braid Beard. "Where
will we bury the treasure?"

I stepped forward. "Maybe I can help!" I shouted over
the wind. "I think I know the perfect digging spot!"

When the storm was over, we rowed back to shore and buried the chest. We drew a map so we could find the treasure again, but I don't think I'll need it.

After that the pirates repaired the ship and got ready to set sail.

Before they left, Braid Beard handed me a flag and said, "You make a fine pirate, Jeremy Jacob. Guard that treasure well. We'll be back to get it soon enough."

"Soon enough!" the crew repeated.

"And if you ever need us," Braid Beard added, "just run the Jolly Roger up yonder pole."

"Up yonder pole!" the others shouted.

And maybe I will, but not today....

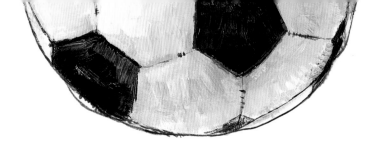

I have soccer practice.

For my brother, Mark, with whom I spent many hours in pretend
adventures; for Gail, who loves him; and especially for
Samuel Jess, the newest pirate in the family — M. L.


Hoist a tankard to Adam and Lizzie —
thar be a lot o' pirate in them two! — D. S.

Text copyright © 2003 by Melinda Long
Illustrations copyright © 2003 by David Shannon

Requests for permission to make copies of any part of the work
should be mailed to the following address: Permissions Department,
Harcourt, Inc., 6277 Sea Harbor Drive, Orlando, Florida 32887-6777.


www.HarcourtBooks.com


Library of Congress Cataloging-in-Publication Data
Long, Melinda.
How I became a pirate/written by Melinda Long; illustrated by David Shannon.
p.  cm.
Summary: Jeremy Jacob joins Braid Beard and his pirate crew
and finds out about pirate language, pirate manners, and other aspects of their life.
[1. Pirates—Fiction.] I. Shannon, David, 1959— ill. II. Title.
PZ7.L856Ho 2003
[E]—dc21    2002006308
ISBN 0-15-201848-4


M O Q S U V T R P N L


The illustrations in this book were done in acrylic on illustration board.
The display lettering was created by Jane Dill.
The text type was set in Packard Bold.
Color separations by Colourscan Co. Pte. Ltd., Singapore
Printed and bound by Tien Wah Press, Singapore
This book was printed on totally chlorine-free Enso Stora Matte paper.
Production supervision by Sandra Grebenar and Ginger Boyer
Designed by Barry Age and Scott Piehl